BARTHOLOMEW ROBERTS' SPIRIT

JEREMY MCLEAN

POINTS OF SAIL
PUBLISHING

Points of Sail Publishing
P.O. Box 30083 Prospect Plaza
FREDERICTON, New Brunswick
E3B 0H8, Canada

Edited by Vicky Brewster
https://vickybrewstereditor.com/

This is a work of fiction. Any similarity to persons, living or dead, is purely coincidental… Or is it?

ACKNOWLEDGEMENTS

Thanks to all my friends and family for their constant support, and the fans who have stuck by for so long.

TABLE OF CONTENTS

1. PROVERBS 28:1

"Hard to port! Don't let them escape!" Hank shouted, his hand outstretched over the quarterdeck railing.

The helmsman gritted his teeth and flung the great wheel of the *Fortune* to the right. Mates relayed Hank's orders down the line on the bustling ship. Though their voices were hoarse from the constant shouting and the salt air, they hollered above the din of the crashing waves and booming cannon fire and cracking black powder.

A surge of brine from the deep shot up over the starboard side of the ship, making the sole slick. As the men ran to change the rigging and adjust the sails, they slid and reached for the handholds, but never fell on that wet surface that was their home.

The mist of that salty swell brushed against Bartholomew Roberts' face as he watched their prey change course. His concentration did not allow him to enjoy that refreshing caress, but it would not be the last time he would feel it, so all was not lost.

"Ready starboard!" Roberts bellowed. His voice too was hoarse from the hours of chasing and the salt that seemed to cling to the throat, but he had no trouble making his voice carry across the whole ship. He stood tall, a modern-day Goliath some might say, and he had the tone to match.

The men not in charge of the rigging readied small cannons on the starboard side of the ship as a mate took the order below to the main gun deck. They would not have a clear shot, but it would be enough to punch a few holes at their enemies stern.

The ship, French by the flags it flew and the name *Maîtresse* emblazoned on the side, was being commanded well enough, but Bartholomew could tell the one in command was an inexperienced coward. They flew at the first sight of the *Fortune*, well before they had even dropped the black, and despite being chased for half a day and having the guns, they never fought back. If they had, they might have stood a chance. As it was, they were full of holes and taking on water.

The wind chopped against *Fortune's* sails, making them crack as the billowing mass snapped against the yards. *Fortune* tacked into the wind, so there was no avoiding the sails luffing lazily as they momentarily lost their power.

They were mimicking the *Maîtresse* and trying to keep close. The *Fortune* was a smaller, faster, and more ma- noeuvrable ship, but they had been beating North-West against the wind for hours and only now made some headway to fire the cannons.

Now that they'd come about, *Fortune* was just about ready to fire starboard, and the crew were just waiting, itching for the order.

Roberts raised his hand in the air then brought it down in a fierce chopping motion. "Fi—" Roberts stopped be- fore finishing the command as a flurry of movement took his attention.

On the *Maîtresse* the sails were being trimmed. Roberts thought they were attempting to somehow turn the ship around and give *Fortune* their broadside, but the manoeu- ver would be impossible with such a tight curve. After waiting, his hand still transfixed in the air as though stuck along with the half-uttered command, he saw them strike their colours. The proud French flag of blue and gold was taken down as the ship moved forward on inertia alone.

Their pride stripped away willingly, the crew of the French ship furled their sails fully and let their ship slow until only the force of the waves beneath were moving them. Roberts ordered his crew to follow suit, but at a distance.

"You think it some deception?" Hank asked through a laboured breath.

Roberts shook his head. "Have you ever known a Frenchman to throw down his pride for deception?" he said with a deep chuckle, expecting no true answer from his first mate. "Given our chase, I think these men are simple cowards who've given up, but there's no need to give them our broadside."

Hank nodded. "Agreed. I'll have the crew remain at the ready and have us circle around with a wide berth." After a moment's pause to see if Roberts would object, Hank went back to his post and shouted orders to the crew.

Roberts kept a close eye, both naked and through a spyglass, on the surrendered French ship. A merchant ship, and by the look of it a new one, it had nary a nick or a scratch on the hull save what damage the *Fortune* had dealt. No signs of discolouration on the wood from weather, no blackened blotches near the gunports from gunpowder, and even the crew looked as green as new-born babes. Roberts could practically see them shaking in their boots as their eyes followed him and the pirates circling the waters.

Despite all the signs pointing to their cowardice and cooperation, it was only after Roberts saw the crew coming up to the weather deck that he felt safe in bringing his ship in close to the other. The gunports were shielded, their cannons reined in and not at the ready, but it would be a simple thing to open them and fire if they had the crew to do so. Looking at the numbers on the weather deck, it would be strange for them to have many more hiding below.

Roberts took his gaze out of the spyglass and looked over at Hank standing nearby at the helm. With a nod, Hank issued new orders to the crew to bring them up next to the French ship. Once the two were close, the crew lashed the ships together before setting down a gangplank.

The rest of the crew of *Fortune* waited for their captain to cross first, all eyes resting on him, all eyes filled to bursting with pride. It was as though the removal of the French merchants' pride became their own; as though that was the first thing they had stolen, the first act of piracy they committed against the enemy before they took more tangible prizes.

Roberts felt that pride too, but he was not one to be swept up in such emotion, and so he took a slow, measured jaunt to the other ship.

The crew of the *Maîtresse* also had their eyes fixed on Roberts, looking up at him as he strode across the gangplank. Tense brows, dark eyes, and twitches at each creak of wood plastered across each of the men on the merchant ship. Those were dangerous eyes. Roberts knew that the fight wasn't over, even now, and he needed to act quickly before the fear seeped into their legs, before the fact that they were cornered and near to the grave sunk in.

Roberts waved his crew over, and they went to the

other ship immediately, all armed and pointing those arms at the French crew.

"Good afternoon, gentlemen," he said loud and long. His Welsh accent gave the saying a merry tone like a song, and his wide smile added to the mirth. "I notice this is a French ship, though I'm afraid I do not speak your beautiful language. Is there any among you who can translate?"

After qustioning once more, a young man stepped forward, and Roberts beckoned him closer before addressing the crew again.

"Today is a pleasant day, so let us keep our business pleasant as well, shall we?" The young man, after a brief pause and a frightened jump, translated for Roberts. Roberts' gaze travelled across the crewmates as he said this, but he wasn't expecting an answer. "Your cowardice today put you here. Perhaps with a little more courage, you could have escaped, but that is not possible now. If you act against us now, you will die. If you stay as you are, you will live another day. Am I understood?"

The young man passing along Roberts' message glanced up at him as he wrung his hands, then back to the crew several times as they both waited for a response.

"Speak, men!" Roberts bellowed, causing several of the French crew to jump, including the young man beside him.

The crew understood without the need for another translation, and they finally answered Roberts. Though Roberts didn't know the language, he at least understood knew the general affirmative responses he was given.

In a lower tone, he turned to the young man and asked, "Now, where is your Captain that I may speak with him?"

The young man pulled his hands in close and looked away. "Captain is gone. No captain now."

Roberts shook his head solemnly. However their captain met their end, he doubted it was from any of the cannon fire during their chase. Roberts said a prayer for the man who had died, then gave the young man a warm smile before giving him a light push and pointing him back to the rest of the crew.

"Keep watch over the men. No laxing in your duties," Roberts shouted to his crew. They replied with nods and "ayes" and lifting their weapons up to show they were alert. Now that the battle was over, and a nice rest just over the horizon, they were eager to have the business over without complications.

Roberts issued a few more orders to those who would not be on guard duty, having them search the ship for all the valuables they could find. After the search was delegated properly, Roberts did his own exploring. He found the captain's cabin below deck and began looking through the ledger book, the captain's journal, and the manifest for anything of note. The captain seemed to be working for English debtors and so it was mostly written in English. The rest he was able to surmise through context.

Through Roberts' reading, he came to truly know the extent to which this ship's former captain, and its entire crew, were like newborn babes. The captain made a series of blunders trading from port to port, not taking stock of the local region's needs and necessities.

He had tried to sell a shipment of tobacco he received from one of the northern Thirteen Colonies in the Caribbean, a short route which could have been profitable if not for it being a location already ripe with tobacco. He only managed to sell a tenth of what he had bought, and at a loss mind you, and didn't have the supplies or funds necessary to sail to Europe where he might have been able to make a profit.

From there, he made the smart decision to trade the tobacco for some sugar rather than try to sell it, but he was swindled judging by the amounts traded. Then, to make matters worse, the crew weren't attentive with the storage of the sugar, and a third of it took on water. He managed to sell the rest to one of the colonies north, then purchased various textiles, which would have come from Britain, for too much by Roberts' estimation. His final note mentioned heading to Trepassey, Newfoundland to sell the textiles.

This too would have been a disastrous move, as the French hadn't been in control of Trepassey for some years. He would have had made a better time of rolling a rock up a hill than dickering with the British colonists for textiles they probably already had.

And to top it all he was attacked by pirates. Little wonder the young captain made the choice he did after all that.

Hank entered through the open door of the cabin, his heavy boots announcing his presence. Roberts looked up from the journal and waved to him before continuing to look through the other ledgers strewn about on the table in front of him.

"Anything of interest?" Hank asked.

"Just the sad tale of a suicidal fool," Roberts replied harshly, then let out a sigh at his rashness.

Hank ignored Roberts' comment, or also didn't think much of the captain who'd left his crew and life behind. "The boys're near finished loading the ship. Wasn't much to take from this lot, but they had fresh food and good clothes."

"And boxes filled with wool blankets and rugs?" Roberts leaned back in his chair as Hank took a seat across from him.

Hank nodded. "You want us to take them?"

Roberts shook his head. "We've nowhere to safely unload them here. I believe we could make better gains farther north."

Hank raised a curious brow. "You've an idea for our next destination?"

Roberts grinned. "Aye, that I do. Trepassey. It's recently switched hands from the French to the British, so there's bound to be much trade going on in its shores."

Hank chuckled. "We colonists are useless without our luxuries from the motherland." Hank began to rise from his seat. "I'll let the crew know we're to depart."

Roberts waved the comment away. "Sit and have a drink with me. The crew will be busy for a bit longer yet."

Hank sat back down as Roberts went into the drawers of the captain's table, and sure enough, there was a bottle of some alcohol and glasses. He poured some for the two of them and passed a glass to Hank. The two drank. It looked, smelled, and tasted cheap, with a harsh, bitter note alongside the burning of a drink meant more for the effects than for recreation, but it was still enjoyable in the right company.

The two sat in amicable silence for a few moments as Roberts reflected. Over Hank's shoulder, Roberts could see the crew bustling about, comparing their finds and talking. The chatter was overpowered by the sounds of boots against wood and the lapping of the waves on all sides of the ship.

Roberts' thoughts turned to what had led the merchant

captain to his untimely end, and on what steps led Roberts to be here as well. He thought on his friend Talib, who he was powerless to help, but was freed by a pirate, Howell Davis. Even after all that Talib had been through—the loss of his wife, the enslavement—he never lost his hope.

Roberts felt it odd that Talib would keep his slave name, Bartholomew. He said it was because he wasn't truly free and kept it as some sort of penance, but Roberts still didn't understand. *The penance was not being strong enough to save your people, your wife, wasn't it, Talib?* Roberts thought. *And now, I'm Bartholomew.* Roberts smiled despite himself, thinking that he had drunk perhaps a bit too much.

After a few more minutes, and half of the drink gone, Roberts leaned forward and broke the silence. "What do you think was going through the captain's head?"

Hank looked at Roberts for a moment, then off to the side as he pondered the question. "Probably thought we were the bad sort of pirates. The red flags, the murderous bunch that they tell stories of to scare children. Might have thought it was a better way to go."

Roberts nodded at the soundness of this line of thought, but in his mind, it didn't seem to match with the contents of the man's journal. The way he talked of his own failures, and how little recourse he would have if his debt collectors came to task for him, it seemed as though this was one failure too many.

"This may be… in poor taste," Hank began.

"No, please, continue. I should hope at this point there would be no barriers between us."

Hank nodded, his face solemn and sombre. "Have you ever… had the inclination?"

It took a moment for Roberts to understand Hank's meaning, and when he did, he leaned back in his chair again. "I think any man alive who would say 'no' to that question is a liar or a simpleton." Roberts finished his drink and rose to his feet. He walked over to his first mate and laid a hand on his shoulder briefly as he tried his best to express something that words could not to his longtime friend. After a moment, he spoke. "Let us leave this business behind us and move on to Trepassey."

Hank nodded again, and this time he wore a small smile. "Aye, Captain."

Roberts had commanded his crew to leave enough food and supplies aboard the *Maîtresse* so they may reach safe harbour alive and well, then set sail north for Trepassey. He also lifted the normal restriction of drinking on deck and on duty, in moderation, and so the men were full of good spirits in more ways than one as they sailed.

After their lengthy chase and the paltry goods seized from their quarry, it was pleasureful for the crew to have a break on their voyage. The weather cooperated with them along the way, giving them wind in their sails for most of the journey, save one peculiar day when the wind simply stopped.

On that day it was clear on all sides, and they could see no approaching ships, and so Roberts decided that would be a day of rest. Roberts looked at his journal and noticed that the day itself was also a Sunday and he chuckled to himself.

The crew rested to the full extent of their ability, drinking, playing games of cards, singing, and eating a proper meal. With no wind, there was no fear of any ship reaching them where they were, and so even Roberts had a few more drinks than typical. Before long, his booming voice was singing the loudest.

After their day of rest, they continued onward to Trepassey with all haste. The winds were once more in their favour, and they reached the harbour without incident. What awaited them was the perfect harbour for merchants, with a natural cove-like shape, it gave just enough room for ships coming and going. This resulted in almost two hundred ships within the harbour, the majority being fishing vessels, but over twenty were larger merchant ships.

This cove shape also meant it was the perfect harbour for pirates. With a bit of work, a single pirate ship could hold the harbour, and none could escape without risking a wave of cannon fire—unless the ships worked together, which is difficult in the best of times, let alone with crews who hardly know each other. There was no escape against a properly outfitted and experienced crew.

And Roberts had such a crew in spades.

"General quarters! Raise the black!" Roberts shouted. "Load port and starboard! Bring to the sails. Show them our colours men, and let's see who answers the call!"

At the end of each order, the crew shouted back an, "Aye, Captain!" and the last left a devilish grin on each man's face.

The black flag of the *Fortune*, a new one depicting Roberts standing on two skulls, was raised to the topmast where all could see. Then the sails were taken in, and their momentum stopped, but the crew held the lines at the ready, waiting for the order to take to the wind.

"Fire a warning shot," Roberts commanded Hank.

"Single fire, starboard!" Hank shouted, and a mate relayed the order below deck.

After only the briefest of moments, one of the cannons off the right side of the ship fired. The heavy sound knocked against Roberts' chest, and he moved to the balls of his feet to stay stock still with his hands behind his back. Smoke rose from the front starboard, lingering and twisting in the air around the ship, clouding the view of Trepassy and the many ships in the harbour for a small, fleeting breath.

After the sound of the cannon fire was gone, there was silence. The only sound heard was the gentle breeze whistling its discordant sound across the deck and the off-beat accompaniment of the lapping waves.

Then the small chirps of chaos swelling to a cacophony met Roberts' ears. Alarm bells rang out soon after, drowning out most other noise in its wake. The bells were loud and piercing, meant to hit the part of the ear that you simply couldn't ignore, and the irregular clanging made it all the harder to disregard.

As Roberts watched and waited with his crew, he grew more and more disgusted by what he saw. The crews of the other ships were abandoning their posts, some jumping into longboats, others fleeing to the sea and swimming to shore. One after the other, they each abandoned their ships to get away from the *Fortune* and the mere thought of danger.

"What cowardly fools," Roberts whispered to himself.

Then, to the eastern side of the harbour, a cannon shot boomed into the air. Roberts' heart thundered in his ear, the shot of energy one feels before the beginning of a fight surging through him, and the hairs on his neck prickled. He took out his spyglass and aimed it to where the cannon fire came from.

On the eastern side of the harbour, close to where the *Fortune* made its stand, was a two-masted brigantine that was bigger and longer than the *Fortune*. Looking it over, it also had more guns than them and could prove a worthy opponent.

Alas, Roberts' hopes for some courage were misplaced, as he could see the crew of this other ship dragging one of their mates from below deck off and away. The mate looked angry and tried to fight against the other men, but they overpowered him.

That young man must have gone against orders to flee, Roberts thought.

After that single act of brave defiance, there were no others. The rest of the one-hundred and seventy-two ships in the harbour were emptied of their crew, who fled to shore to hide with the citizens of Trepassey.

And then it was as quiet as the moment just prior to the panic. The streets were clear, the doors and windows of the town shut, shuttered, and secured. The only sound was the friendly wind at Roberts' back, and the waves jostling the ship.

Roberts was stunned into silence by what he had witnessed. In all his days, he never thought this would happen. Judging by the looks on his men's faces, he wasn't the only one shocked. If the merchant crews had attacked together, even just two of them, they may have overwhelmed the *Fortune*. Many could have escaped, had they simply set off in the chaos, had they simply attempted it. It wouldn't have been worth the trouble of a chase; Roberts probably would have let some go.

After Roberts' shock and anger at the men's cowardice fizzled out, the absurdity crept in as he took stock of the number of empty ships in the harbour. Then excitement bubbled up from his gut into his chest. It swelled until he couldn't contain it any longer, and he burst out laughing. Roberts laughed in heaps, arching his back and resting his hands on his stomach as though trying to contain the good humour he suddenly felt in himself.

At first, the crew were stunned at Roberts' laughter, and then after a few tepid glances to their neighbours, the men caught the same excited feeling as their captain. In an instant, the crew were in hysterics.

Roberts shuffled over to Hank as he reached out and grabbed the man's shoulder for support and his attention. "Did... did you see the one that tripped... and tumbled over the side?" Roberts made a circling motion with his hands, and then he and Hank both burst into fresh laughter.

The unexpected humour continued for a full minute before the crew tried in earnest to gather their wits about them and contain themselves.

Roberts wiped tears from his eyes as he chuckled in small fits before he finally came back to himself and addressed the crew. His voice, though composed, still held the elation and laughter now confined in his chest. "Men, let us not waste this golden opportunity we have been given. So, let us be bold like lions and take what the Lord has provided us," Roberts said with a flourish and a wave of his hand towards the ships in the harbour waiting for them.

2. APPLES

Hank stepped up from the longboat onto the pier of Trepassey and took stock of his surroundings as the twenty men who joined him came onto solid ground.

On the pier, it was slightly harder to see the total number of ships abandoned in the harbour, but there was almost no break in the line they made. Hank could barely see the line of the horizon through the dense clustering of ships both large and small drifting in the waves. The wind and the sea were pushing all of them to and fro, and those not anchored down slowly drifted towards each other at a slow pace.

The town itself was large enough to warrant the number of ships in the harbour, but it appeared to still be growing. There also seemed to be signs of battle, worn cobbles, new planks of wood in the middle of the dock at shore, and new buildings mixed with the old. Hank didn't pay much attention to current events, but his captain mentioned the town recently changed hands from the French to the English. Before that, it must have been a contested area.

With the crew ashore, Hank led the group to the market just off the dock. The small stands the minor merchants and locals used were abandoned. Fresh fruit, fish, meat, animal hides, and other small oddities any sailor couldn't do without were left in their haste.

"Go fetch me an apple, would you kindly?" Hank asked one of the crewmates as he nodded his head towards a nearby cartful.

The crewmate took a moment to follow Hank's gaze, then smiled as he jogged over to the cart of fresh ruby red apples. He scratched his chin as he searched for the best, gathering an armful of them to bring back.

Hank had first pick, thanked the crewmate, and took a hearty bite. The bite was sweet and tart with an explosion of juice which fell down his chin. Though simple, it was delicious and a welcome retreat from the salty meat they had to endure for months on end aboard their ship.

Judging from the looks on the other crewmates' faces, they were getting just as much, if not more, enjoyment from the apples than he was.

"We should bring some back for the men. Grab us the cart and load the longboat."

With wide smiles, a few of the crew went to task, taking the whole cart back to the pier where they had secured their longboat. Apples spilled off the sides as they rolled down the small mound above the cart, leaving a trail behind the laughing, giddy crewmates.

Returning his attention to the town, Hank looked at the windows of the shops and homes that faced the harbour. He could see the telltale signs of onlookers trying to remain inconspicuous. Slight bends in the blinds, the smallest crack to let in just enough sound, and even a child here and there full-faced looking at them before a swift hand pulled them away.

Hank nodded to himself, thinking it was good that they were listening. It made what was coming next easier.

"Alright boys, we're about to get started," Hank said over his shoulder before pulling out a pistol. Hank loaded the gun with black powder, but not with a lead ball, aimed off into the distance, and fired. The sharp crack bounced and echoed off the walls of the houses as it travelled across town.

After the sound dissipated and Hank was sure he had even more of the town's attention than before, he spoke into the silence. "Attention, citizens of Trepassey," he said in a booming voice for all to hear. "We are not here for you. We only lay claim to the ships and the cargo the cowardly merchants who stalk your shores left behind. If you leave us to our business, you will be left alone, and alive." Hank let the words hang in the air as he searched the windows and doors for any activity. "Now, for the captains of the twenty-two merchant ships, I would have words with you. Come out now if you want a chance to save your ships."

After Hank finished, there was silence in the town once again. He knew there would be a delay as the captains debated whether to follow the words of a pirate and risk their lives. They were without spine, but Hank was sure that the threat to their ships would move their feet eventually.

"Someone bring me something to sit on, would you? And relax, we might be here for a spell," Hank said as he readied his pistol once again, this time with a lead shot loaded.

One of the crewmates rolled over a nearby barrel and stood it up for Hank to sit on. Hank grabbed another apple off the ground from those that had fallen off the cart, wiped it off, and sat down on the barrel.

Hank took his time eating his second apple, savouring the flavour he so rarely got to enjoy, as he and the other crewmates waited for the captains to come out of hiding.

17

The crew decided to relax as well, some sitting on the ground nearby, others taking their pick of the abandoned wares the vendors had left behind, and a few others polished their weapons or made sure their rifles were loaded and ready.

Slowly, people exited various nearby businesses into the street leading to where Hank and company were gathered. Around fifty people in total came out to meet with Hank, far more than the number of merchant ships, and many of them had weapons in hand. Hank thought it might have been an attempt to intimidate the twenty men he had brought with him, but it would be a foolhardy one.

"I suppose I'm going to have to teach these boys a lesson," Hank whispered to himself. He whistled, and the crew who had been lounging about came back to join him where he sat. He didn't rise from his seat, nor did he stop eating his apple, as the fifty men approached.

Before Hank could say anything, a few of the men holding weapons charged in unison, one of them headed straight for him. The crew of the *Fortune*, battle-hardened as they were, knew it was going to happen and struck back. One crewmate blocked the man coming for Hank and stabbed him through the stomach, and the others were dispatched just as easily. As swiftly as it began, it was over. Four were dead, none of them pirates.

The ease with which the merchants' men died soured the thought of attacking from the remaining forty-some. Hank too hadn't moved from his spot, and his casual attitude no doubt sealed it.

Hank took another bite from his apple and began speaking after signalling to one of the crew. "Thank you for joining us gentlemen," he said with a mouthful of apple. "My name is Hank Abbot, first mate of the *Fortune* captained by Bartholomew Roberts. Perhaps you've heard of him?" Hank gazed into the eyes of those thronged about him and saw some knowing looks of fear, and a few he thought might be admiration. "I trust you all understand why we're here. If you want to keep your ships intact, you'll do as we say." He waited a moment to see if there were any objections, but none came. "First, you're going to give us each of your names and which ship you belonged to."

The crewmate Hank had signalled rolled another barrel nearby along with a small crate he placed overtop, and then set down an inkwell and a piece of paper. After weighing the paper down with rocks, he looked expectantly towards the gathered crowd.

"W-why?" one of the men asked.

It wasn't a defiant question, but one borne of confusion. Hank simply looked down towards the four dead men, then back up to the man who asked 'why'.

There were no further questions.

Each captain lined up in a row as the others, their mates or villagers, stood off to the side. Most of the men looked afraid and jumpy, but Hank noticed one young man who appeared to be angry. His face held a deep contempt and shame, and it wasn't always directed at Hank or the other pirates.

The whole process was smooth and efficient, with each captain being more than amicable given the circumstances. After they were finished, the captains returned to the other crowd of people and waited.

Hank nodded, satisfied with the outcome. "I thank you for your cooperation, gentlemen. Now, down to business. If you wish to save your ships, then you are to report to our ship, the *Fortune*, after you hear the sound of a rifle. Those who fail to do so will have their ship burned at once."

At the end of Hank's declaration, there was a small clamour from the captains and others in the crowd. Their greed took over their wits, making them forget the four that had died so easily not moments before. It seemed to be momentary, but then one of the captains stepped forward.

"This is outrageous!" the captain blared. "Just take the cargo and leave these—"

The crack of Hank's pistol cut through the noise of the captain and the men behind him. The captain who had objected stepped forward once, fell to his knees, and slumped to the ground dead.

Hank waited for a moment, letting the silence permeate the air once more as the smoke from his pistol wafted around him like a shroud before disappearing on the breeze.

"Who was his second in command?" Hank asked as he pointed at the dead captain. A young man stepped forward and raised his hand. "Congratulations," Hank said, "you're captain now. Give your name to my man here." The young man nodded and rushed over to update the list, nearly tripping over himself as he did so. Hank looked over the rest in the crowd. "Any other objections?" There were none. "Good. After the sound of a rifle, report to the ship the *Fortune*. Do not keep my captain waiting. Understood?"

Earlier

Roberts and Hank both set foot on the largest ship in the harbour. It had minimal guns, but it was even larger than the brigantine that had fired upon them. At first, Roberts thought it could make for a nice replacement ship for the *Fortune*, but upon seeing it more closely, he knew what kind of ship it was.

"Prepare food and water, and lots of it!" Roberts commanded. "And bring over some prybars."

Roberts and Hank went below deck to the small area divvied up for the crew and captain at the stern near the ladders. The next level down went below the water line for bilge access. There was enough room for a crew of around fifty to one hundred, just barely enough to run a ship of this size, and then the rest of the ship was blocked by thick timbers and a heavy locked door with no airflow to speak of.

Despite there being no way for air to escape, Roberts could smell the rank stench of disease, filth, and death beyond that door. It was a smell he had been familiar with at one time, a smell he had grown accustomed to, a smell he learned to forget until he could forget it no longer.

The wooden door had a large iron lock keeping it closed. Hank pulled out a pistol and began aiming it at the lock, but Roberts stopped him.

"Too dangerous," Roberts said, trying to limit the words and the amount of time he had to intake the smell. "Might injure someone."

Hank nodded, and the two waited for a crewmate to bring a prybar. Roberts took it in hand, set it against the lock, and using his giant form, he snapped the lock with one mighty blow.

With the door open, there was nothing to stop the smell from inside, and it nearly knocked Roberts over. The crewmate who had brought the prybar wretched and had to leave.

Inside, dozens of eyes, fearful like fawns, looked at Roberts and Hank. There couldn't have been less than two hundred and fifty men and women in that part of the ship, huddled so close together there was barely enough room to breathe.

And of all the things that Roberts thought in that moment, he was thankful that this was one of the ships where the slaves were allowed to stand. The ship he had been on in the past kept them on wooden bunks two feet apart up to the overhead, and some were worse than that. Two feet was a luxury.

The men and women were all halfway, or closer, to death. Frail from malnourishment, sickly, and with scars or lesions covering their bodies from fresh injuries.

Roberts tried his best to adopt a warm and reassuring face. "Come, come out. You're free now," he said.

At first, no one moved. Then one woman, naked save for a cloth covering her genitals, reached for his hand. Roberts took it gently and led the woman out, pointing her to the ladder leading above deck.

After the woman, the rest of those aboard came more quickly, but still with caution and fear in their eyes. After some time, they had all those who were able on the weather deck where Roberts' crew fed and gave them water to drink. Afterwards, Roberts had his surgeon help the sick and wounded as best he could, and brought food and drink to those below who couldn't stand.

Of those there, he found eighty long dead from the voyage, rotting near the corner where the slaves were meant to relieve themselves. The sight disgusted Roberts. As many times as he had seen it, as many times he had freed those enslaved, he lost no anger over time. His righteous fury was everlasting in the face of these atrocities.

After a moment to calm himself, he joined the abled on the weather deck. The slaves were drinking and eating, some helping those weakened even from the short trip above deck. They were eying Roberts' crew warily.

"Do any here speak English?" Roberts asked. He had a dozen or so former slaves aboard his ship who he could call on if needed, but he knew from experience his message would be better received if it came from one they trusted. He waited a moment before repeating the question, then one of the men raised a hand cautiously. Roberts bade the man join him. "Do any here know how to sail a ship? Are there enough to escape on your own?"

The man, though thinning, looked a fair bit healthier than many of those who survived. He looked over the other former slaves, then shook his head. "No enough to sail. No enough for big ship."

"How many?" Roberts asked, raising his hands and motioning with his fingers. The man motioned back twenty, then waved his hand as if to say it wasn't a firm number. Roberts thanked the man and motioned for him to go back to having his fill before he turned around to Hank. "Thoughts?"

"Our ship isn't big enough to bring them all with us, and even if we took this ship as well, it would mean putting them back in the hold again."

Roberts shook his head. "And then we would have a slaver and be worse off than before in terms of battle power."

Hank leaned back and scratched the back of his head. "If we wanted to take them comfortably, even the brigantine wouldn't do. We'd need to split to two ships. Even with the twenty who can sail helping us, it wouldn't be enough."

"They're too weak as it is at the moment. We need to train some, and we need them to regain their strength back."

Hank scoffed as he looked off towards Trepassy. "We need time is what we need. Time we don't have."

Roberts closed his eyes and stroked his chin for a few moments as he mulled over the problem. After a while, he opened his eyes again. "I have an idea to buy us some time," he said. Hank arched an eyebrow. "We're going to have a little fun with these cowardly captains."

"What are we going to do?"

The captains who had abandoned their ships were meeting together after the pirates' first mate and crew left. They had brought along many of their most trusted crewmates as well, some of whom were now dead.

"What can we do? You saw what they are capable of." Some in the crowd nodded and shared some words of agreement. "These men are cold-blooded murderers, and they're far more capable than any of us."

The debate went on for a time, with each of the captains going back and forth about whether they should follow along with the pirates to try and save their ships, questioning whether it was a trap, and wondering just what the reason behind wanting to meet with them was.

Eventually, a young man in the crowd had enough and

stepped forward. "You bunch of cowards could have ended this immediately if you'd had any spine," he said.

The captains all stopped and went silent as they turned their attention to the young man. One of the captains stepped forward, bowing his head slightly in deference. "Apologies for my crewmate's remarks, gentlemen," he began, before turning and uttering, "James, now is not—"

The young man pointed at his captain sternly. "Don't you even start. You're the worst of the lot. We have the biggest ship and more guns than that puny sloop. We could have taken those pirates ourselves if you hadn't ordered everyone to abandon ship."

The captain was caught off guard by his crewmate's rebuke and couldn't think of a response. The young man pushed his captain aside and addressed the others again.

"And all of you are the same. Most of your ships have guns, and not a one fired. You didn't even try to escape with your ship. Sheep to the slaughter, all of you." With each remark, the anger and volume of James' voice grew.

After he finished, there were a few with shameful faces looking down at the ground, but many returned the anger back.

"And what would you have us do?" one of the gentlemen said in a proper British accent.

"Go meet with the pirate if you want to save your ship. Throw down your heads in shame and beg for his mercy. Or don't," James said with a shrug. "Just don't go on about it like a bunch of children told off by their teacher. Be men about it."

Before the captains could argue with James any longer, there was the distinct sound of a rifle from the harbour. All eyes shifted to the harbour, where the pirate ship *Fortune* stayed drifting.

James walked off in that direction, not looking back at his or the other captains, to prepare a longboat. With determined resignation, the forty-some in the crowd joined him, and they were soon off to the pirates' ship to meet with its captain, Bartholomew Roberts.

Once aboard the ship, the captains and mates were surrounded on all sides by pirates. One of the pirates was on the opposite side of the ship to them, sitting in a chair next to a table with what could only be described as a genteel set of teapot and cups.

The pirate himself was a giant. Even sitting down, he was an imposing figure that struck fear into the hearts of those in attendance. He delicately picked up one of the teacups in his massive hand, raised it to the gathered captains and mates, and said, "Welcome gentlemen!" with a wide smile. "Would you care for a cup of tea?"

3. AFTERNOON TEA

Bartholomew Roberts poured himself a fresh cup, paying those around him no mind as he carefully measured out the smallest bit of sugar to his liking. The sugar was taken from one of the merchants' ships, whose captain would be standing somewhere in that crowd.

Roberts took the cup up to his nose, took a deep inhale as he sampled the notes of spice and black tea leaves and then took a sip. He let out a drawn sigh of satisfaction as he peered over the crowd. "Many thanks to the captain of the *Heaven's Tackle*, you've brought in some exquisite tea." He took another sip. "Or perhaps I should say *heavenly*?" he said with a deep laugh.

Looking over the expressions of those in the crowd, it was difficult to say which of them was the *Heaven's Tackle* captain as several baulked at his jesting. He had hoped for as much. Though he knew with his stature he was an imposing figure, he hoped his demeanour would keep them off guard.

One in the crowd, however, seemed unfazed. A young man stepped forward and crossed his arms. "So are you going to tell us why we're here, or not?"

Roberts looked over at the young man and recognised him as the only one who had dared to fire a cannon at their ship while the others were escaping. Of all those in attendance, that youngster was the only one who held a shred of courage, and so Roberts held a small bit of respect for him.

"Straight to business. I like it," Roberts said as he grinned. "You are all here for a test. You will tell me of your business dealings, where you come from, what you have done to get to where you are, and why you fled your ships today. If I like what I hear, then your ships will be spared."

Before Roberts could call his first captain for questioning, the crowd of them rose up in a clamour. Their voices blended together in their rush to speak with him, all of them trying to figure out what it was they had to say to save their ships. If not for Roberts' men having their rifles trained on the group, they would have probably dared to clamber around him in their eagerness.

Roberts waited until their questions died away, sipping his tea and ignoring them as he did so. Once there was silence again, he turned his attention back to the men. "I will not be able to say just what answers I am looking for to forestall the destruction of your ships; all I will say is to answer truthfully."

"Who do you think you are? God?" The young man from before asked. His arms were folded, and he had a contentious look on his face.

Roberts let out a hearty laugh. "I'm not judging their souls, boy. I'll leave that to Him." He got up and walked over to the young man, and despite Roberts standing a head and a half above him, he didn't cower. "What's your name, boy?"

"James Skyrme," he replied.

"A good name," Roberts said. "I have been pirating for several years, and I haven't met a merchant yet who hadn't deserved what was coming to him."

"You're just a thief. Exodus 20:15, 'Thou shall not

steal'."

Roberts raised an eyebrow, not expecting to be the one on the receiving end of a bible quote. Roberts shrugged and shook his head. "If what I'm doing is unjust, then I too will be judged accordingly, after I take my last breath." Roberts pointed to one of the men on the ship, the frail former slave who could speak a little English. "You see that man there? He only speaks a bit of this language, but he was able to tell me how the people who brought him here stole him and many of his family away in the night. That was after they raped his wife, who died of illness on the trip here." Roberts took a breath as he felt his anger rising. That was not the way he wanted to present himself to these men. "'The thief cometh not but for to steal, and to kill, and to destroy: I am come that they might have life, and have it in abundance.'" Roberts made a flourish as he quoted John 10:10, raising his arms towards the slaves aboard that they had just freed.

James gritted his teeth. "So, you don't think yourself God, but instead a saviour?"

Roberts shook his head. "No, my boy. I don't *think* of myself as anything. I *am* a pirate." He leaned forward and spoke in a whisper that only James and a few close by could hear. "Some time ago, I decided to take on the spirit of a departed friend of mine and vowed to free any slaves I could in his name. If God considers me a thief for stealing back that which was stolen, then so be it. I will hope that the good that I am doing will serve to absolve me of my sins."

Roberts turned away from James and motioned to one of the crewmates. The crewmate nodded and made a signal towards the harbour. Afterwards, he looked through a spyglass, and then said, "It's done."

"Good," Roberts replied. "To the captain of *Brooken*, you have already failed, and so your ship is no more. You may remain ashore the next time I call on the other captains."

The captains looked amongst themselves, trying to identify the captain of *Brooken*, when one of them rushed to the side of the *Fortune*. They all followed the man with their eyes, then they too were looking off towards the harbour where the largest ship was already burning. The fire was growing rapidly, taking over the ship until the light from it was too bright to look at.

The captain of *Brooken* fell to his knees in tears, shock stealing the words from his mouth. Not only had his slaves been freed, but his ship destroyed in front of his eyes.

Roberts thought that this must have been how the captain of *Maîtresse* must have felt, but he shrugged it off and went back to the table where his tea waited for him.

Roberts took a sip of his tea and waited for the captains to turn their attention back to him. After a few moments, after the peripheral shock had worn thin, they turned around to face their captor once again, and this time with a fresh, new type of fear in their eyes.

"Would the captain of *Resolute* please join me?" he said, motioning his hand towards the seat in front of him.

After the interrogation with the pirate captain, the merchant captains and mates went back to a pub in Trepassey to discuss what to do next. They were all given some basic introductory questions from Roberts, but most of what they did for business was left out, which meant that would come later.

"We need a plan," one of the captains suggested.

"What kind of plan?"

"One where we all get out of this with our ships intact, and maybe more." The captain had a sleazy grin on his face as he sat down in the middle of the throng of captains. "This pirate is a godly man, so I say we appeal to his godly nature. Tell him about what good we've done. Tell him about all the charity we do, the sort of sob story he's sure to eat up."

James' captain spoke up next. "I don't know about this," he said. "He doesn't seem like the type that should be lied to. What if he finds out?"

The first captain raised his brow. "Well, that's why we're here making sure we have our stories straight, innit? 'Sides, that negro-lover ain't got his head on straight, so he won't know the difference. Now, here's the plan."

The captains all came close together, listening to the first strong voice that spoke up rather than thinking for themselves. It made James sick, and so he spat and left the tavern to find his crewmates. He knew what to do about the pirate problem, and he knew his mates would have his back when the time came.

4. *GOOD FORTUNE*

Over the course of three days, Roberts continued his interrogation of the merchant captains. Each morning they fired a rifle, and each morning like clockwork they arrived on his ship. Roberts' goal was to stall for time until the slaves were fit to sail, and so he only asked the captains a few questions each as he drank tea. Some questions had to do with their trade, some with their background, and others about the crewmates aboard their ships.

Though Roberts was at times talkative, a trait his crew could attest to, talking with these merchants was tiring. Each one of them was too eager to please him: calling him 'sir', wringing their hands and bowing their heads, giving more information than he had asked for and being extra polite. It was sickening how false they were in front of him. In some it was fear, in others he could tell they had an open disdain for those he'd freed but were trying to hide it to appease him.

After the captains had left on the third day, Roberts let out a long sigh and stretched his hands into the air, arching his sore back. He looked out to the harbour with all the empty ships still floating about. Most of the fishing ships and those who were not anchored down had clustered together on one side of the harbour from the drifting waves, leaving the harbour looking barren and deserted.

Hank came over next to Roberts and leaned forward on the starboard railing. "The crew just finished stripping the merchant ships. We can leave a hefty amount of cargo for the men we freed, and still have a goodly amount for us to sell ourselves. There's almost too much to choose from."

"Aye," Roberts said. "I thought as much. I don't expect us to have such good fortune as this again. Our enemies have done half the work for us."

Hank turned around, and half sat on the railing as he looked at Roberts. "Speaking of the cowards, how is your tea time?" Hank had a small grin on the corners of his lips.

"Exhausting. How much longer until the men are trained and well enough to sail?"

Hank shrugged and shook his head. "They're learning quickly enough, and teaching select people specific tasks is more effective, but it's no small feat to sail a ship. I would want another week, maybe two for them to be fit enough to sail on their own."

Roberts felt a sour taste in his mouth at the prospect of having to entertain talking with the merchants for another seven-to-fourteen days. With that much time on their hands, however, they could do some much-needed repairs on the ship or...

"Perhaps we should use this time to procure ourselves a better ship," Roberts said. He pointed to the largest ship in the harbour, second largest prior to them burning the slaver. It was a two-masted brigantine with ten more guns than the *Fortune* had, a total of twenty-six.

Still half sitting on the railing, Hank looked over his

shoulder at the ship Roberts was pointing at. "Aye, that ship would do us well. The extra cannons could provide us better protection. Lord knows we can't expect this to happen again," Hank said with a smirk on his face as he motioned around him.

"Luck comes but once to the unexpectant, and not at all to those who desire it." Roberts stroked his chin for a moment. "I think our new ship deserves a fitting name to match the circumstances around us taking it."

"What were you thinking?"

"How about *Good Fortune*?"

"One—no, two ships approaching from the South-East, Captain!" one of Roberts' men shouted from the port side of their new ship.

Roberts and Hank both looked at the crewmate, then each other, before they dropped what they were doing to look over the side of the ship. Some of the other crewmates joined in as well.

The two ships on approach were still a few hours out from Trepassey, but there was no denying that they were headed their way. The crew was halfway through bringing their belongings over to the *Good Fortune*, having yet to secure the cargo and supplies they had taken from the other ships in the harbour. If they hadn't been so focussed on switching to their new ship, they may have spotted the approaching ships sooner and had more time to prepare.

Roberts took out his spyglass and looked through it. He couldn't make out the flags or the size, but he could tell they were both loaded with cannons. One was a shade bigger, probably an escort for the smaller ship.

"What should we do?" Hank asked. "If we beat to, we could have the ship loaded and ready before they arrive and be on our way."

Roberts gritted his teeth at the thought of running, but it was the safest course of action. Without knowing the size and number of guns the ships had, it was difficult to know how they would fare in a battle.

He looked over his shoulder at the men and women they had set free, watching the sea with fearful eyes. They could take them all on their new ship, but they wouldn't get very far laden down with that many bodies, and that's before taking into account the amount of food they would need and didn't have, or how crowded it would be with over four hundred aboard a brigantine.

"No, we'll take a gamble and fight. I want the guns loaded and at the ready on both the *Fortune* and *Good Fortune*. We might need them both."

Hank nodded and said, "Aye, Captain," before he turned to issue orders to the crew aboard their new ship. He sent runners off on one of the longboats to inform the crew on *Fortune* to ready for battle.

"Now the question is, how do we fight them?" Roberts said out loud.

Roberts pondered the question. Now that the men they had freed were slightly trained, they could help on *Fortune* to do some small manoeuvers, while the bulk of the crew in *Good Fortune* took the fight to the ships. But if they did that it wouldn't be long before they realised the smaller *Fortune* was an easy target and sink it.

If they could get just one of the ships in close

enough, the two could fire broadsides at them and might be able to take out the larger escort ship. But how would they lure them in that close? They would of course need to take down their black flags, but the rest of the ships in the harbour were empty of crew. If they saw two ships with a full complement then...

The idea struck Roberts at once. He called for a runner to pass along new orders, and then they prepared for battle.

As the two ships approached, the cannons were loaded and ready, but the two ships under Roberts' command kept the sails lashed and the anchor lowered. When they needed to, it would be a simple thing to cut and run, loose the sails to enter battle.

As the ships approached, most of the crewmates aboard both pirate ships went below deck, with only a scarce few staying atop to watch their approach. Those above hid behind the corners of the ship or the cargo lying about so as not to be seen by the enemy ships.

Roberts stayed above deck, watching as the two ships rose and sunk, their bows crashed against the waves as they approached. When they came closer to harbour and the sails were taken in, the crashing turned into a small chop. The crewmates of both ships were too busy gawking at the myriad empty ships in the harbour to man the sails, and they let the ship go forward on the tide.

The air was still and thick with anticipation. Sweat soaked Roberts' brow as he peered at the approaching ships. He could feel his heart beating sharp and swift in his chest, a thunderous drum that sounded so loud but was only his to hear. He couldn't help but lift his hand up, wooden and stiff, and place it just beneath his throat.

He took a few deep breaths as he watched the larger escort ship inch forward, closer and closer to where they could give them broadsides. It felt as though they should have been close enough already, but they needed to be closer.

Then Roberts locked eyes with one of the enemy crewmates. Roberts' heart stopped, and he clamped his teeth down hard. There was no way the man on the other ship could see him. Was there? He was looking at the ship with eyes unaided by any instrument. But if Roberts could see him, then the opposite was true.

Roberts pried his eyes away from the enemy crewmate and noticed the ship was in position. For a split second, he looked back at the man who spotted him and he noticed a hand outstretched pointing at Roberts—but it was too late.

"Fire starboard!" Roberts shouted so loudly he felt that his other ship, the *Fortune*, could hear as well.

A frantic few heartbeats later and cannon fire thundered from below deck. The noise echoed across the harbour, bouncing off the houses and back before the iron had even smashed into the other ship. The asynchronous snapping of a dozen dozen wooden planks exploding into bits all at once came next as smoke crept up from starboard and billowed on the weather deck. There was a short lull during which Roberts could hear the screams of the panicked and injured before another wave of thunder from the other side of the harbour sounded off.

Roberts ducked down to safety behind the quarterdeck ladder, but nothing happened. Then he realised the second wave of cannon fire had been from the *Fortune*, not the enemy ships. Roberts came out from behind cover as his crew returned above deck, and he saw the larger ship was taking on water, and before long would sink. The two broadsides had crippled it to the point there was no saving it.

Before he could let himself relish in the plan working, he looked south to the smaller ship that the larger one had been escorting. Without protection, it would be easy to take, provided they didn't let it escape.

"Loose the sails! Cut and run!" Roberts shouted before pointing at the small merchant ship. "Don't let that ship leave the harbour!"

The crew went to work, letting the sails down for the wind to take them. Hank ran to port, raised his cutlass above his head, and slammed it down against the anchor's rope. He severed it in two with such force that his cutlass embedded itself in the port railing. The rope tethering the ship in place fell into the drink, and they were free to move.

The small merchant ship had only dropped their sails again by the time *Good Fortune* had begun turning around and into the wind, the suddenness of the attack on their escort no doubt slowing their reaction. *Good Fortune* was beside them before they could turn themselves around. The pirates threw grapples across, and the two ships were secured together.

Gunfire erupted across both ships; the pirates shooting at the merchants trying to cut the lines holding the ships together, and the merchants returning defensive fire.

Black powder, the smell of it burning the nostril, the

sound of it piercing the ears, the feel of it kicking the musket against the shoulder. It was all at once old and familiar and exhilarating, and at the same time new and strange and terrifying to Roberts. He was both accustomed to the feeling of battle, and yet it was like sailing into the chaos of a typhoon. There was no telling what would happen, and it was both thrilling and frightening in equal degrees.

The ships were pulled together, partially by the tidal forces, and partially by the grapples. Once close enough, the pirates aboard *Good Fortune* braved the hail of lead to cross the gap and take the fight to the other ship's deck.

Roberts joined his crewmates in leaping across, not looking to the small bit of sea jumping up at them between the ships, and landed on the enemy ship. He drew his cutlass, and from the looks of those aboard, looking up at him and his towering frame, they were afraid. This too, this fear in the eyes of his enemies, was a familiar, exhilarating, and terrifying feeling.

Once Roberts began cutting down the defenders two at a time, it became clear to the rest that continuing the fight was futile. The rest of the crew surrendered and dropped their weapons on the deck of their ship.

Roberts wiped his brow of sweat as he took a few deep breaths and watched the crew of the merchant ship herded to one side. He also noticed some of the men of his own crew were injured and being tended to. Hank was bandaging his arm as blood trailed down it, and his chestnut hair was matted to his forehead. Hank looked up and saw Roberts there, and flashed a devilish grin before going back to his work.

"Men, I want this ship's valuables stripped and

moved to *Good Fortune*. She's a touch bare at the moment and needs some new cargo, wouldn't you agree?"

The pirates chuckled and said, "Aye," as they went to work.

In little time they took all the valuables from the merchant ship, leaving a scant few things for those left. The haul they got was better than most of what they were able to salvage from the merchants who'd abandoned ship. Roberts thought it might have been because this ship only just arrived to Trepassey, unlike the others.

As the pirates moved the cargo over, the remaining men from the escort ship had made their way to the merchant ship on longboats. A few of them were armed but threw their weapons away when commanded by Roberts' crew.

The escort ship was still sinking, so there was no way to salvage any of its cargo in time, but Roberts wasn't concerned. With the limited space aboard *Good Fortune* and the other ships they had already pillaged, it wasn't much of a loss.

As the crew were finishing bringing the supplies from the merchant ship over, one of Roberts' crewmates came to get him. "Captain, that kid from before is here. Says he wants to speak with you."

Roberts arched his brow, not remembering who it was his crewmate was referring to. He walked over to the side of the ship, where the young man named James Skyrme was waiting in a longboat with his hands in the air.

Roberts grinned. "Bring him aboard. Let's see what he has to say."

Jeremy McLean

"Fire! Fire in the harbour!"

Shouts from the street awoke the merchant captains and crew in Trepassey, and they all left their temporary lodgings to see what the commotion was about. A cursory look at the houses nearby showed no signs of fire or smoke, but the townsfolk rushing to the harbour told the story at once.

In the harbour, the remaining twenty merchant ships were burning. The fires raged so intense that one could feel the heat of the blaze even on land. The only thing stopping it from spreading to the other abandoned ships and threatening the houses were the anchors pinning the ships together, but the ropes wouldn't last long.

The captains of the merchant ships watched as their entire livelihoods went up in a plume of black smoke in front of them. They stared for silent minutes as the citizens shouted and ran to work, taking precautions to save their houses should the fiery cluster of ships move closer inland.

A runner came to them after a time with a letter, and the captains gathered to read it.

To the captains of the merchant ships in Trepassey,

> *You will no doubt find your ships already burning at the arrival of this correspondence and wrongfully come to the conclusion our agreement was broken. This is not so, as I shall explain.*
> *Throughout our acquaintances you have all of you lied in*

one form or another. Whether about your business dealings, or otherwise. You attempted to deceive in an effort to save yourselves, but instead, all of you together assured your ships' destruction.

I shall leave you with these parting words from Revelation 21:8:

"But the fearful and unbelieving, and the abominable and murderers, and whoremongers, and sorcerers, and idolaters, and all liars shall have their part in the lake which burneth with fire and brimstone, which is the second death."

Bartholomew Roberts

"I must thank you, young lad," Roberts said as he raised his cup of tea in the air. "Without your help, not only would we still be stuck in Trepassy biding our time to train the former slaves, but I may have missed out on teaching some of those merchants a lesson."

James Skyrme raised his cup as well, and then the two took a few sips. "I couldn't stand by as those bunch of cowards slipped by, lying and cheating again. I thought I'd rather be a pirate than work for any of them again, and some of my mates agreed."

Roberts smiled. "Well, I am certainly glad for the change of heart. If I had to talk with them for another week longer, I'd have needed some stiffer tea." The two men laughed together for a moment and sipped at their not-so-stiff tea once again. "So, have you considered my offer?"

Skyrme lowered his cup onto the saucer nearby. "I have, and I'll accept it. But won't some of your crew be angry?"

Roberts shook his head. "I've already consulted them on the matter, and they agreed to it. All that was left was to see if you wanted the same."

Skyrme raised an eyebrow. "I suppose it's settled then."

Roberts took the last sip from his teacup and rose from his seat. "Are you ready?"

Skyrme nodded and joined Roberts. The two of them headed towards the exit of the *Good Fortune's* cabin, but Skyrme stopped short.

"There was one matter I forgot to ask you about. Would I be able to rename the *Fortune* to the *Ranger*?"

Roberts grinned. "Why, of course," he said as he slapped the young man on his back. "You're her captain now. Just treat her well, that's all I ask."

Skyrme smiled back at Roberts. "Aye, Captain."

Roberts and Skyrme headed out of the cabin and up to the weather deck where some of the crew had gathered. Skyrme was sworn in on the Pirate Commandments under oath with Roberts' bible and then announced to be the new captain of the ship formerly known as *Fortune*. After the ceremony, and a small celebration, Skyrme and his mates headed back to the newly named *Ranger* in a longboat.

Hank joined Roberts in his new cabin after the festivities and the two shared a drink.

"After all this interesting business you'd think you'd be sick of tea," Hank commented.

Roberts laughed. "One would think." Roberts took a

sip and admired the flavour. "You are right in that this has been an interesting few weeks."

Hank nodded. "Mayhaps this was our best haul yet, if we don't include your raid of the Portuguese ships."

Roberts grinned and nodded as well. "Yes, that one would be difficult to topple. I suppose I'll simply have to try harder next time." The two had a small chuckle and raised their cups at the prospect. "I know the crew had a discussion already about it, but I do hope you're not angered that I made that young man captain. I feel your daily council is something I cannot do without."

"No need to trouble yourself on it. I don't want to be captain. Too much responsibility, if you ask me," Hank said, and waved his hand as though waving away smoke.

"You sound like someone I once knew."

Hank leaned forward. "Aye, I knew that man too," he said. "I think his name used to be John, as I recall. And that same man became the best damn captain there was. I'd have it no other way."

The two smiled and raised their cups once again before enjoying a few minutes of congenial silence as the ship bobbed up and down against the waves.

Once more, Roberts' thoughts turned to his old friend Talib, and he wondered if he was doing right by him. Whether it was righteous to steal from the wicked he knew not, but he would continue on regardless. *Once I take on my old name and meet with you again, Talib, I'll know then whether what I've done is righteous. Until then, this shall be my penance.*

When the tea was finished, Hank rose from his chair. "Suppose I'll have a bit of a rest," he said. "Where are we headed to next, you figure?"

Roberts leaned back in his chair and looked off into space. "I suppose we should unload our cargo somewhere south. Once our guests are fully trained, we can secure them their own ship elsewhere to head back to their homeland in."

Hank raised his brow. "South? Back to the Caribbean?"

Roberts nodded, and he couldn't hold back a grin. "It's been some time since we've been there. I'm interested to see what's happened since we've been gone."

Hank grinned as well, the both of them knowing that the true purpose was to check in on an old, estranged friend. Roberts hoped beyond hope that that old friend might be a different man than when he last left, and if so, he hoped beyond hope that they might rekindle that friendship once again.

Proverbs 10:28: "The patient abiding of the righteous shall be gladness..."

THE END

OTHER BOOKS BY THE AUTHOR

The Pirate Priest Series:

BARTHOLOMEW ROBERTS' FAITH

BARTHOLOMEW ROBERTS' JUSTICE

BARTHOLOMEW ROBERTS' MERCY

BARTHOLOMEW ROBERTS' SPIRIT

The Voyages of Queen Anne's Revenge Series:

BLACKBEARD'S FREEDOM

BLACKBEARD'S REVENGE

BLACKBEARD'S JUSTICE

BLACKBEARD'S FAMILY

The Collection Series:

BLACKBEARD'S SHIP (Includes Books 1&2 of The Voyages of Queen Anne's Revenge & The Pirate Priest)

BLACKBEARD'S BLOOD (Includes Books 3&4 of The Voyages of Queen Anne's Revenge & The Pirate Priest)

ABOUT THE AUTHOR

JEREMY IS CURRENTLY LIVING IN NEW BRUNSWICK, CANADA WITH HIS WIFE HEATHER, AND THEIR TWO CATS, NAVI AND THOR.

Jeremy's first foray into the writing world was during a writing competition called NaNoWriMo, where the goal is to write a certain number of words in the month of November.

After completing the novel he started, and some extensive rewrites, he felt it was worthy of publishing and self-published his first novel, Blackbeard's Freedom in September, 2012.

After writing over ten books under two names, his passion for writing hasn't wavered over the years, and hopes to one day make it his primary career.

Let everyone know what you thought of his novels by leaving a review. He loves getting feedback on his books, and loves to hear from fans of his work.

Want to pirate one of Jeremy's novels? Visit http://www.mcleansnovels.com/free-book-link for a free copy of one of his books.

www.ingramcontent.com/pod-product-compliance
Lightning Source LLC
Chambersburg PA
CBHW071237170626
46809CB00008BA/3097